Richard [Scarry's Little]

Bedtime Book

Random House 🏠 New York

First American Edition. Copyright © 1978 by Richard Scarry. All rights reserved under International and Pan-American Copyright Conventions. Published in the United States by Random House, Inc., New York, and simultaneously in Canada by Random House of Canada Limited, Toronto. Originally published in Great Britain by William Collins Sons & Co. Ltd., Glasgow and London. Copyright © 1977 by William Collins Sons & Co. Ltd. ISBN: 0-394-83967-6. *Library of Congress Catalog Card Number:* 78-55298. Manufactured in the United States of America   1 2 3 4 5 6 7 8 9 0

The Three Fishermen

Lowly, Huckle and Daddy were going
fishing.
"See you catch some nice fish," said
Mommy.

Their little motorboat took them far
away from shore.
"This looks like a good spot," said
Huckle.

Daddy said, "Throw out the anchor,
Lowly."
Lowly threw the anchor out . . . and
himself with it!

Lowly climbed back in, and Daddy began
to fish.

Soon Daddy caught an old bicycle. . . .
But he didn't want an old bicycle.
He wanted a fish.

Daddy fished some more, but he still didn't catch a fish.

Then Huckle fell overboard.
Wouldn't you know that something like that would happen?

Daddy pulled Huckle out. Why, look!
Huckle has caught a fish in his pants!

But Daddy didn't catch anything.
He was disgusted.
"Let's go home," he said. "There just
aren't any fish down there."

As Daddy was getting out
of the boat, he slipped . . .
and fell!

Suddenly he began to yell loudly.

Aha! A fish was biting his tail.
The fish was trying to catch Daddy!
It is good that Daddy has a strong tail.

Now Lowly is the only one who hasn't
caught . . . But wait a moment!
Lowly has taken off his hat.

Do you see what is under it?
A FISH! Very good, Lowly.

Yes, there you see three
very good fishermen!

Wow!

The Accident

Harvey Pig was driving down the street.
(Better keep your eyes on the road,
Harvey.)

Well! He didn't keep his
eyes on the road and he
had an accident.

Sergeant Murphy came riding along.
"Everyone get onto the sidewalk,"
he said. "I don't want anyone
arguing in the street. You might
get run over."
So everyone got onto the sidewalk.

And just in time, too!
Rocky was driving his bulldozer down
the street.

"I'm very sorry about that," he said.
"I guess I wasn't looking where I was
going."

All right, now. Keep calm, everybody!
Here comes Greasy George, the garage
mechanic.

Greasy George towed away the cars,
and the motorcycle, and all the loose
pieces.

"I will fix everything just like new,"
he said. "Come and get them in about
a week."

Greasy George worked and worked to
make everything just like new again.
Stand back, Huckle! Don't get too
close to him!

Well, Greasy George was certainly telling
the truth. When everyone came back
everything was NEW all right!
I don't know how you did it, Greasy
George, but I think you got the parts
a little bit mixed up!

The Three Sitters

Mother Bear saw Wolfgang, Benny, and
Harry walking past. She ran out and
said, "My house is in a shocking mess.
I've got to clean it from top to
bottom. Will you please baby-sit
with Robert while I go shopping for
some soap?"

If Mother Bear had stopped to think
for a moment, she might have worried
about leaving Robert with those three.
(Do you think they know how to baby-
sit?)

Wolfgang, Benny, and Harry agreed to
stay and play with Robert while Mother
Bear went shopping.

After a while they got tired of
playing.
"I have a good idea," said
Harry. "Let's make some fudge."
(I don't think Mother Bear
would approve of that. Do you?)

When they had finished mixing everything together, they poured it into a pan.

(Do you think
they *really* know
how to make fudge?)

Then they all sat down at the kitchen
table to wait for the fudge to cook.
Gurgle, burble! Burble, gurgle!
Something seems to be bubbling over!

POP! ! !
The oven door burst
open. The fudge had
exploded!

RUN! RUN! FOR YOUR LIVES!

Lowly ran to the telephone.
"HELP!" he cried.
"The fudge is
rising! Our
house is sinking
in fudge!"

Look out, everyone!
Here come the firemen.

Soon every bit of fudge had been
washed out of the house—
along with a few other things.
But LOOK! Who is that coming?
Why, it's Mother Bear.
Hurry up, fellows!

Put everything back in place!

"I have never seen my house looking
so spick and span," said Mother Bear.
"I think we should have a party.
Who would like to make some fudge?"

Lowly said, "I think it would be
better if you made it, Mother Bear."
And so she did. And everyone ate the
best fudge in the cleanest, spick-est,
span-est house ever!

The Unlucky Day

Mr. Raccoon opened his eyes.
"Wake up, Mamma," he said.
"It looks like a good day."

He turned on the water. The faucet broke.
"Call Mr. Fixit, Mamma," he said.

He sat down to breakfast.
He burned his toast.
Mamma burned his bacon.

Mamma told him to bring home
food for supper.
As he was leaving, the door fell
off its hinges.

Driving down the road, Mr. Raccoon
got a flat tire.

While he was changing the wheel,
his trousers ripped.

When he started off again, his engine blew up and wouldn't go any farther.

He decided to walk. The wind blew his hat away. Bye-bye, hat!

As he ran after his hat, he fell into
a manhole.

Then he climbed out and bumped into a
lamp post.

A policeman yelled at him for bending
the lamp post.
"I must be more careful," he thought.

"This is turning into a bad day."

But he didn't look
where he was going.
He walked right
in front of
Warty Hog.

Then he bumped into Mrs. Rabbit
and broke all her eggs.

Another policeman gave him a ticket
for littering the sidewalk.

"I think I had better go
home as quickly as
possible," thought
Mr. Raccoon. "I don't
want to get into
any more trouble."

He arrived home just as Mr. Fixit was leaving. Mr. Fixit had spent the whole day finding new leaks.
"I will come back tomorrow to fix the leaks," said Mr. Fixit.

SOAP

Mrs. Raccoon asked her husband if he
had brought home the food she asked
for. She wanted to cook something
hot for supper.

Of course, Mr. Raccoon hadn't, so they
had to eat cold pickles for supper.

After supper, they went upstairs to
bed. "There isn't another unlucky
thing that can happen to me today,"
said Mr. Raccoon as he got into bed.
Oh, dear! His bed broke! I do hope
that Mr. Raccoon will have a better
day tomorrow, don't you?